WAITING FOR SUNSHINE

A SUSSEX CRIME NOVELLA

By Isabella Muir

Published in Great Britain
By Outset Publishing Ltd

Published March 2020

ISBN:1-872889-29-8

ISBN:978-1-872889-29-0

www.isabellamuir.com

Cover photo: by Leon Biss on Unsplash
Cover design: by Christoffer Petersen
Map of Tamarisk Bay: by Richard Whincop

'Laughter is sunshine, it chases winter from the human face.'
Victor Hugo 1802-1885

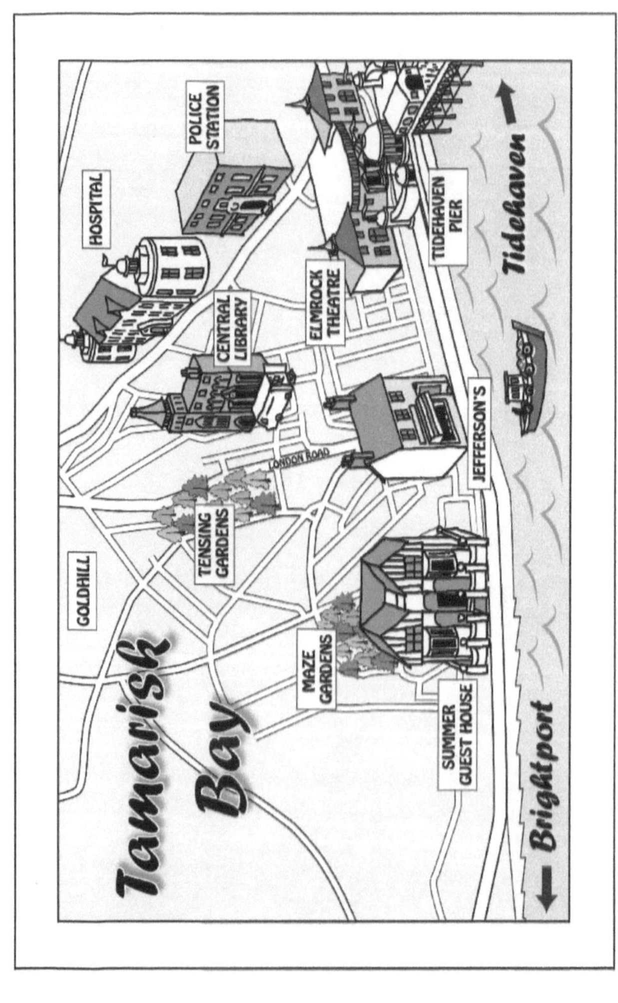

Tamarish Bay
GOLDHILL
HOSPITAL
POLICE STATION
CENTRAL LIBRARY
ELMROCK THEATRE
TENSING GARDENS
LONDON ROAD
MAZE GARDENS
SUMMER GUEST HOUSE
JEFFERSON'S
TIDEHAVEN PIER
Tidehaven
Brightport

1

You would think that as a journalist I'd find it easy to tell the story of my life. I spend my working week telling other people's stories, reporting on minor and major misdemeanours, digging around the back story to discover where the blame truly lies. Yet somehow, when it comes to unravelling my own memories, I get into a tangle. It's the sort of mess you might find after a kitten has been playing with two balls of wool. If I could lay out those balls of wool, side by side, perhaps I would have a chance to see things clearly. Trouble is, the memories I think are real keep getting mixed up with the ones I'm given - the stories that Mum and Gran repeat - as if they remember a whole set of events that somehow passed me by.

One thing all three of us agree on is the day I was introduced to my dad. It was my birthday - I'd reached the grand age of three. Gran had made me a new dress of bright yellow cotton and knitted a yellow cardigan to match. The cardigan was more like a jacket, the wool thick and scratchy on my skin. But then, when you have a February birthday, it's important to be prepared for all weathers. Over the years I've celebrated the day in snow, rain and storms, even sunshine on occasion, but never warmth - that would be too much to ask for.

Mum had promised me a cake. I didn't appreciate then just how much of a sacrifice would need to be made for the cake to become a reality. Food rationing had been in place since 1940 and, although the war ended just around the time I was born, by 1948 rationing was far from over. This all meant I had never tasted cake made with fresh eggs, plenty of sugar and butter - all ingredients that were available in abundance before Hitler decided to invade Poland, sending the world into chaos.

So there I was, sitting at the kitchen table, in my yellow dress and cardigan. To accompany the birthday cake, sweetened with carrots instead of sugar, Mum had made shortbread from potatoes instead of flour. As Mum has never been the most skilful of cooks (despite following Gran's recipes to the letter) I'm certain the home-baked goodies wouldn't have looked or smelled quite as appetising as when Gran made them. There was bread and jam too, the jam made from Gran's home-grown blackberries. Jars that had sat in the larder from before the war, a time when adding pounds of sugar to the shopping list presented no problem. We had been eking out the jam and with just two jars left, the presence of one of them as part of my birthday spread signified a celebration of sorts.

I remember reaching across the table for a slice of bread, only to have Mum smack my hand.

'You've to wait, Libby. See, I've laid two more places. We'll start when everyone is here.'

Gran and I always sat opposite each other at mealtimes, with Mum at the head of the table. But now another place had been set. I don't think I wondered too much about who it might be. My main anxiety was that whoever it was should hurry up, so I didn't have to spend too much longer looking at the teatime spread without being able to touch any of it.

Then the back door opened, and in walked a man. The first thing I noticed about him was his smile, which resulted in creases appearing not just at the side of his mouth, but around his eyes too. So much mischief in those eyes, even though back then I didn't know what adult mischief might entail. But I was certain I'd never seen a man smile in such an all-encompassing way, as though there was nothing wrong in the world and everything was possible. I'd seen polite smiles on our doctor's face when he listened to my chest, and hopeful smiles when I accompanied Gran to the shops on a Saturday and she promised to have our bills settled by the end of the month. This man's smile was nothing like that. Plus, it was a stark contrast to the expression on my mum's face, which reminded me of someone who has sucked a sour lemon by mistake.

'Libby, this is Adam,' Mum said.

I don't recall if he said anything just then, but I can hear his loud laugh when I announced, 'Can we start eating now?'

The stranger meant nothing to me, except that his arrival signalled the start of teatime.

I'm sure it was during that tea party when it was made clear to me that Adam was my dad, although I can't remember much of the detail. I'm not sure what Mum or Gran told me, or how they worded it, but I know that by the end of my party I was excited to realise that this man was related to me in some way. Whenever we talk about it now, which is rare, Mum's version of that day is that Adam turned up late and couldn't even be bothered to stay to read me a bedtime story. It was the first of many occasions when my dad fell well short of what my mum expected.

Whereas I got much more than I had hoped for, particularly as up until then I didn't even know I had a dad. It had just been Gran and Mum and me and that had been fine, with my gran, Phyllis Frobisher, as the captain of our little family, calming troubled waters with her wise words.

Adam's arrival that day brought more than just birthday surprises into the house. The teddy bear and jigsaw puzzle certainly won me over, as did the little black-and-white photo of himself that he pressed into my hand. But best of all was the laughter he brought into our kitchen. It was as though he had an invisible wall around him, protecting him from the disapproving looks from Mum, that she made no attempt to hide. Nothing was going to shift that smile from Adam's face. And when he called me Primrose and picked me up from my chair and spun me around in his arms, I knew life would never be the same again.

2

A ten-minute walk up through the twittens and alleyways of Tidehaven Old Town brings you to *Lavender Cottage*, the picturesque, if somewhat dilapidated cottage that was home for Mum, Gran and me.

I was born there, weirdly enough, in the same bedroom I slept in through to my teenage years. It was a noisy house in a quiet lane. The noises didn't emanate from us, but from the creaking floorboards and the rattle of old wooden windows, which provided so much draught most days that there was barely a need to open them. We didn't have a view of the sea from our lane, but a short walk downhill brought us onto the shingle beach, right beside the fishing boats.

Roll forward a few years from my third birthday and Adam had continued to drift in and out of our lives, although definitely more out than in. Whenever he visited he never failed to bring sunshine with him, regardless of the weather. He would arrive, often early morning, when I was still in my pyjamas, pouring cornflakes into my cereal bowl. Once he was there, sitting beside me, I was too excited to eat and often he would slide my bowl towards him and munch his way through the contents. On the rare occasion he stayed long enough to take me out for an adventure, we would walk together over the Fire Hills, his long stride making it impossible for me to keep up with him. Even on a calm day the breeze would scuttle across the hilltop, blowing my hair into my eyes and making me catch my breath. I usually spent the return journey sitting on his shoulders, enjoying a bird's-eye view across the gorse-covered sandstone cliffs, down into Tidehaven Harbour.

On those walks I had no questions for him, I was content enough just to be in his company. He never said much, choosing instead to hum tunes or sing songs. Perhaps music gave him a freedom that language didn't offer. Whatever the reason, his lilting, husky voice became the backing track to many of my dreams.

During those early years I accepted Adam as an occasional but joyous addition to our little family. He was like Christmas Day, but one that might arrive at any point through the year, and one that couldn't be relied on to arrive at all.

Just once I challenged Mum with a direct question. I didn't mean it as a criticism, I only ever wanted to try to understand.

'Why is Adam always so happy and you are always so miserable?'

I don't recall the answer, even if there was one. It was just as likely she would have shooed me away with a wave of her hand, telling me to eat my tea, or tidy my toys before bedtime.

I longed for Adam's injection of laughter, that energetic Christmas spirit, so that when it seemed like forever since Adam's last visit I would pester Mum.

'When is Adam calling round? Where is he?'

She was never able to answer because she didn't know, which made me idolise him even more - not only was he a man of fun, he was also a man of mystery.

It was about halfway through my ninth year when I began to look outside the confines of Lavender Cottage, with a questioning eye. Imogen Rutherford was my best friend. On my first day at primary school she sat beside me and from that moment we became inseparable. Most weeks I would visit the Rutherford's house, sit at the tea table with her mum and dad and brother and absorb the chatter.

At home, conversations mostly went over my head. Gran would either talk about her day at school, or her garden. Phyllis Frobisher had been a teacher at Grosvenor Grammar forever, teaching several generations of the community and securing herself a place as an integral part of the fabric of Tidehaven and Tamarisk Bay. Of course, one day she would have to retire and it was accepted the school would be the poorer for it.

When Gran wasn't teaching, she pottered in her garden, which ran around all four sides of the cottage. The front comprised a paved footpath edged with lavender, leading from the gate to the front door. I always made a point of brushing my hand through it whenever I passed, sometimes grabbing a handful of the flowers and stuffing them into my pocket so that I could savour the sweet heady perfume throughout the day. To the left and right of the cottage Gran had dug deep flower borders, filling them with every kind of cottage garden flower, arranging them in order of height, ensuring there was colour for every season. The back garden was reserved for vegetables; wigwams of runner beans, tidy rows of carrots and onions, with pots here and there introducing scented herbs, such as marjoram and chives.

Mum, on the other hand, rarely set foot in the garden, and certainly not if there was digging or weeding to do. Her interests seemed to extend no further than her work as a nurse. During the war, as a teenager, she had volunteered as a nursing auxiliary, and once the war was over she did her nurse training and continued to work in the local hospital, mainly covering night shifts, so that between her and Gran there was always someone around for me.

As a result, the conversation around our kitchen table rarely involved topics where I could join in, as neither gardening nor nursing piqued my interest. Most of the time, I felt as though I was being talked at or over. So, on the day Mr Rutherford first asked for my opinion I merely blushed and stuttered. I didn't know until then that something I said could possibly be valid or of interest.

'What do you think of our young Queen then?' he said. 'No sooner than she was crowned and she set off all around the world, thousands of miles she's travelled, just imagine some of the sights she's seen.'

I knew nothing about the Queen. I'd never been to London and I'd never stopped to imagine what it might be like to live in a palace. I had a vague memory of Mum and Gran listening to the Queen's coronation on the wireless and feeling annoyed by the presenter's voice droning on for what seemed like hours.

Nevertheless, I came home from the Rutherford house that day, determined to discover all I could about 'current affairs'. The next time Mr Rutherford asked me a question I would be prepared with an intelligent and comprehensive answer. I asked Mum if I could buy a newspaper with my pocket money and she laughed, as if I was joking. Regardless, once a week I bought a copy of *The Times* and was immediately daunted by pages filled with nothing but small print, with very few pictures. My reading ability was above average for my age, but I still had to borrow Gran's dictionary and look up almost every other word.

At first I selected short articles, with relatively interesting headlines. I read about a rail crash at Sutton Coldfield. An express train had taken a sharp curve too fast and come off the rails, with seventeen people killed and forty-three injured.

A few days later at the Rutherford house I raised the subject, just as Mrs Rutherford handed me my plate of beans on toast.

'It's very sad about the train crash, isn't it?' I said.

'More than sad for those families, young Libby,' Mr Rutherford said. 'But you have to stop and ask yourself who is to blame.'

I hadn't given any thought to the implications, not for the bereaved and not for the driver. That was when I realised there was more to current affairs than just the words on the printed page; there were the stories behind the words. Every event had consequences that rolled on far into the future.

No surprise, perhaps, that as an adult, a newspaper journalist was the only occupation I ever considered. The lessons I learned back then, as a ten-year-old, still stand me in good stead. Each time I read a headline and the first few paragraphs beneath it, I treat the words like the taster from one dish of a banquet, with all the flavours and textures of a whole host of other dishes just waiting to be discovered.

3

After several weeks of reading *The Times*, gradually becoming familiar with the language of grown-ups, I longed for Adam to call round so I could share my new insight with him. It had been months since his last visit, Christmas came and went, and my tenth birthday was approaching. Most years, he had turned up on or around my birthday, always bringing a present, which was never wrapped but became the most treasured of all my gifts, even if it was little more than a new hair ribbon.

My ninth birthday was in 1954, rationing had ended and to celebrate the fact, as well as the fortunate timing of my birthday falling on Shrove Tuesday that year, Gran suggested we have pancakes for my birthday tea. Mum decided to *'push the boat out'*. We didn't just have pancakes for tea, we had them for lunch too, on account of the day falling during half-term. The sweetness of sugar and the citrus tang of lemon enticed me to eat so many on that occasion I felt pretty sick for the rest of the day.

That year Adam didn't visit until well on into the summer. We spent the afternoon together. He took me to Tidehaven Pier and we passed an hour or more playing the *'roll a penny'* machine, putting any winnings straight back in and walking out with the same amount of money we'd walked in with. Adam bought ice-cream cornets and laughed at me when I got it all over my nose and chin.

I told Adam about the birthday pancakes and vowed that by my tenth birthday I would be more sensible, as proof I was nearly grown up. He didn't make any promises, but I had a good feeling he would be there on the day itself.

Instead, the weather conspired against me. Early in February 1955 the country froze, with snow blocking roads, even rail services being cancelled. It was so bad that across the country, in the worst areas, Royal Air Force planes were used to help deliver food and medical supplies to people who were stranded.

So, when there was no visit from Adam - not before my birthday, on the day itself, or for weeks after - Mum and Gran exchanged looks that weren't difficult to read. One night when I was tucked up in bed, supposed to be asleep, I strained my ears to hear their conversation.

'He's a drifter, a dreamer,' Gran said. 'Wasn't that always the attraction?'

'I should never have let him into our lives.' There was a bitterness in Mum's voice that I hadn't heard before.

'No, Audrey, you did the right thing by telling her. Libby needed to know her father.'

'He's no father to her. He lives in a fantasy world, can't hold down a proper job and has no idea of commitment, not to me, not to Libby.'

Despite Mum's accusation, I was certain it was only the snow that was keeping Adam away. But as February ran into March and I continued to read my weekly copy of *The Times*, I wondered if something bad might have happened to my dad. The newspaper reports were showing me that danger lurked around every corner, outside the safe confines of Tidehaven and Tamarisk Bay. It wasn't only train crashes that could take life, there were accidents on the roads as cars increased in number and speed. Then there were the burglaries that resulted in *'grievous bodily harm'* not just to the householder or shopkeeper, but to innocent bystanders.

By the time April arrived I had convinced myself that Adam had been attacked and then run over by a car and was laying injured in a hospital somewhere, unable to talk and desperate for me to visit. I shared none of my anxieties with Mum or Gran. I was certain that Gran's response would be to reassure me. *'The reports you read in the paper, they're extremes, that's why they are in the paper. They're not happening to everyone.'* I could imagine her words.

There was also the possibility that if I had told Gran about my worries, she would release some nugget of information about Adam, something that Mum hadn't told me. I'd reached an age when I wanted facts. The questions started to multiply in my mind.

For a long time I'd kept the photo Adam had given me under my pillow, until I realised the creases that appeared each morning were creating lines and wrinkles in Adam's face. I would slide the photo out as soon as I woke up, hold it in my hand, noticing that Adam seemed to have aged a few more years overnight. So, to protect the only photo I had of my dad, I slid the photo into the front of a diary he had given me for my sixth birthday and kept it in my bedside drawer. I'd not yet written in the diary, savouring the blank pages, promising myself that I would wait until I had words that were worthy enough to grace the pages. But it was during my tenth year when I began to transfer my list of questions from my thoughts to the pages of my diary.

Where do you go when you leave me?
Where do you live?
Why can't I visit your house?

I handled the photo so much that the photo was worn, but the image of Adam I had in my memory never faded. At the age of three, when I first met him, he had seemed like a giant, towering above me. Then, as I grew into myself, I realised that, yes, he was tall, but not in giant-like proportions. In fact, if our odd little family had stood side by side at any point during my tenth year, we would have resembled a set of steps going up the side of a pyramid. Me at the bottom, followed by Gran, who wasn't much more than five feet, then a jump of a few inches to Mum, who in her stockinged feet could rest her chin on the top of Gran's head. Then came Adam, towering above us all, his lanky legs in drainpipe jeans, and a torso so slim that it was difficult to see where he hid his muscles. He sported a quiff, with a Brylcreem gloss, resembling James Dean, and his smile crept into my dreams most nights. I'd often sit in front of my dressing-table mirror and try to recreate that smile. After all, I was his daughter. But the reflection that came back at me resembled a crazy laughing hyena and made me miss him even more.

The months rolled on through 1955 and an ambient spring morphed into a blistering summer - all the extremes of the coldest winter were reversed. Day after day the sun shone and with no sign of rain there were threats of a drought. We learned to save the washing-up water, and it was my job to carry the bowl out and tip it over Gran's precious garden. Some of her flowers and vegetables appeared to thrive in the heat, with sunflowers bolting until their bright yellow faces looked down on me, reminding me of the terrifying plants in *The Day of the Triffids*. It wasn't just the articles in *The Times* that were sparking my imagination.

I had worked my way through Gran's bookshelves, before moving on to the science fiction shelves in the library. Fears that Adam had been run over by a bus or a train were soon overshadowed by a certainty he had been kidnapped by aliens. I read *The Martian Chronicles*, *The Midwich Cuckoos* and on and on, until the reality of my day was lost. The science fiction tales seemed more real to me.

When I sat opposite Gran at the kitchen table, I imagined there was a camera hidden away somewhere, recording everything we said and did. At one point, I even convinced myself Mum wasn't my mother at all, but we were all actors in some kind of weird drama. Whether these were raving delusions, or the average thoughts of a child with an overactive imagination, who knew? With hindsight, I would say it was more likely to be the latter, because when Adam finally turned up early one Sunday morning in August 1955, it was as though normal life had been resumed.

Mum was still in her dressing gown. We'd just finished breakfast, arguing over who should have the last slice of toast, when he pushed the back door open and almost fell in, under the weight of the rucksack on his back.

Mum looked at him, then turned away and busied herself with filling the kettle and putting it on the gas.

'How's my Primrose?' he said, ruffling my hair. It was as though he had never been away. I poured him a mug of tea and he sipped it slowly. Then, before I could ask him anything, he made an announcement. 'I've decided it's time for an adventure. I'm off to explore the Greek islands. Perhaps I'll learn to fish and come back a fisherman.'

Mum acted as though Adam hadn't spoken, as she continued to wash up the breakfast things. As Gran was out in the front garden, tending her plants, I took Adam's hand and led him out into the back garden, choosing a small patch of lawn beside the raspberry canes. Gran had created a framework to support the leggy plants, which provided the perfect screen so that we couldn't be seen from the house. It was like being in our own hideaway.

'Where have you been? You missed my birthday. Again.' I launched straight in, watching his expression. The smile was still there, but there was something else, something in his eyes that told another story.

'Was it a good birthday, Primrose? I'm sorry I missed it.'

'We had pancakes. Like last year, like I told you we would.'

'Then I'm really sorry I missed it.'

He picked up a buttercup and held it under my chin. 'Maybe I should call you Buttercup.'

'I'm not a baby anymore.'

'That's right, you're into double figures and pretty soon you'll be a young woman. Reckon I'll always call you Primrose, though.' He gave a throaty chuckle, as though the thought of it amused him.

'First I thought you'd had an accident…' I paused, trying to second guess what Dad would think about Martians and my random imaginings.

'The thing is, Primrose, I'm going away again.'

'Yes. To Greece. I'll come with you.'

He chuckled again and took my hand in his, counting out my fingers, as if he was silently running through the *'This little piggy went to market'* nursery rhyme.

'I might miss your next birthday, but I'll be back for the one after that, I promise.'

The months stretched ahead of me, great chunks of time, when I would have nothing to look forward to, no spontaneous visits. It would be worse knowing for certain that he wasn't coming, at least when there was a possibility I could hold out hope. I pushed his hand away and stood, turning my back on him.

'Mum's right, you don't care about me.'

'Of course I care about you, Primrose.'

'I'm not your Primrose, I'm not anything to you. You're not even my dad, are you?'

I ran into the house, leaving Adam sitting on the grass. I ignored Mum's questioning look as I slammed the back door behind me and ran up to my bedroom.

Half an hour or so later, after Adam had gone and after I'd made my pillow damp from crying, I crept out onto the landing to listen in on a conversation between Mum and Gran.

'What's he told her?' Gran said, with a hint of conspiracy in her voice.

'I have no idea. Whatever it was you can be certain it won't have been the truth.'

'Do you think she's old enough to know the truth?'

'She's ten years old, Mum. You probably don't remember what that's like, but I certainly do.'

'She's not you, Audrey. She's quite a different character, what's more she's had a very different life to yours.'

'You brought me up and you've had more than a hand in bringing up Libby. So, it's not that different.'

'Your father was around when you were her age, every evening, every weekend. There was a stability that Libby hasn't had. Plus there's that imagination of hers.'

'More like you, than me, then?' Mum's tone resembled that of a petulant child, making me wonder even then who was the adult in our relationship.

I didn't want to hear any more, so I retreated to my bedroom, took Adam's photo from the diary and studied it, willing it to provide me with the answers I longed for.

4

Even though I'd been angry with him, it was after that visit I started to refer to Adam as Dad. I could tell Mum hated me doing it, which made me do it even more. It gave Adam a status in our family I thought he deserved; he was my father and even though I saw him little more than once a year I was certain he loved me.

I knew Mum loved me too, but like most ten-year-olds, I guess I took that for granted. Dad was a man of mystery, drifting in and out of my life. By contrast, there was nothing mysterious about my mum. I'd seen her every day since I was born. She was a creature of routine, which must have made her an excellent nurse.

Most mornings she would come in from her night shift around the time Gran was preparing to take me to school. If I close my eyes now to form a picture of Mum back then, it would be of a woman with bleary eyes, pale cheeks and a drawn look about her, as though staying awake was an effort.

I know now that Mum gave birth to me when she was just seventeen. I can only imagine how impossible that must have been. Illegitimacy is still a taboo subject, but back then, just as the war was ending, it would have been nothing short of devastating. Many young women finding themselves in the '*family way*' would have been thrown out, shunned by their family, facing a life of poverty and disapproval. It's only now that I'm just a few years older than Mum was when she had me, that I realise how few options she would have had. If having a child out of wedlock was impossible, so was getting rid of it. Abortion was illegal - still is. Women who sought a way out, using services outside of the law, risked dreadful infections from dirty instruments, dirty backstreet rooms. Such practices left some women infertile, others lost their life alongside that of their baby.

All in all I was lucky, although as a ten-year-old I didn't feel it. Gran never wavered in her support for Mum and for me and because she was so well respected as a schoolteacher and all round *'pillar of the community'* no one dared to speak against us. At least not in earshot.

But I made comparisons between our lives and Imogen's. I'd go round to the Rutherford house and see her mother in a pretty frock, a style I'd seen Audrey Hepburn wearing in the film posters. The dress showed off Mrs Rutherford's trim waist, the full skirt swishing around as she buzzed around the kitchen. Mum's waist was trim enough to carry out the exact same style. Instead, when she wasn't wearing her nurse's uniform, she donned a shapeless housecoat.

Money might have been part of the problem. Mr Rutherford was a bank manager and local magistrate, his wife had no need to work and there seemed to be no shortage of funds for treats for their family. By contrast, our family was used to managing on a tight budget. Mum and Gran would sit together on a Sunday afternoon, having shooed me into the garden. That was their time to *'do the bills'*. The old Brooke Bond tin that sat on the kitchen windowsill no longer contained tea, but was the store of our 'rainy day' fund. Any coins remaining after all the bills were paid went into that tin.

One evening, when Mum was at work and Gran was watching me brush my teeth, I asked her. 'How come you always put money into that tea tin, but never take any out of it?'

She went through to the kitchen and picked up the tin. She shook it and laughed. 'Look after the pennies and the pounds will look after themselves,' she said, which meant nothing to me at the time and doesn't make much sense to me even now.

But all this scrimping and saving and Mum's complete indifference to anything stylish or *'avant-garde'* made me determined to be the opposite. Whenever I had the chance I would flick through magazines in the newsagent's, trying to memorise the latest fashions, promising myself that one day, when I was earning my own money, I would show everyone just how trendy I could be.

All in all, my outside influences were more vivid and exciting than the world that existed inside the Frobisher household. I was still reading science fiction avidly and, alongside my book reading, I continued to scrutinise *The Times*.

It was in September 1955, just a month after Dad's last visit, when my world started to fall apart. James Dean – my dad's lookalike – crashed his car in California and died. He was twenty four years old. I read the article over and over, not wanting to believe it. The headlines appeared on a Saturday, the day after the car crash, so when I appeared in the kitchen, clutching the newspaper close to me, neither Mum nor Gran barely registered me. Gran was beating some eggs ready to make a sponge and Mum was busy with some hand-washing.

'Look,' I said, wanting them to reassure me that the article was just a hoax. I slapped the paper down on the kitchen table, then tried to pull Mum away from the sink.

'Libby, my hands are wet. What is it? Can't it wait a few minutes?'

'Just look at this, won't you?' I shouted, releasing the frustration I was feeling, holding nothing back.

Gran stopped beating the eggs and looked first at me, then at the newspaper. Finally, Mum dried her hands and turned towards the table.

'Libby, whatever's the matter?'

At that point I picked up the newspaper and ran out into the back garden, throwing myself down onto the grass. I was still there ten minutes later when Gran came out to fetch me.

'Now, what's this all about, Libby? There's no need to get in such a state, is there? It's very sad about James Dean, of course it is. But it's not like you know him. Anyway, he lived all the way over there in America. It's the people around us we need to worry about.'

'That's just it,' I said.

She eased herself down to sit beside me and took my hand in hers.

'How about you tell me what this is really about. What is it that has upset you so?'

'It's Dad.'

'Ah.' It was a simple acknowledgement that she understood, she had made the connection, without my having to explain it all.

'You're worried about your dad?'

I nodded, too confused and emotional to be able to get all the words out in the right order. My brain had been fizzing with all the possibilities for so long, trying to understand the implications and failing hopelessly.

'You miss seeing him, don't you?' Gran said.

'Yes, but that's not the worst of it. It's not like I'm used to him being around.'

'What is the worst of it then?'

'The secrets.'

'Which secrets would that be?'

I shuffled my position on the grass so that I was sitting opposite Gran, rather than beside her.

'You and Mum talk about him when I'm not around, or when you think I can't hear. But he's my dad. I deserve to know as much as you know about him. Otherwise it's not fair.'

I expected a standard response, something along the lines of *'life isn't fair, you'll just have to get used to it'*. But this was Phyllis Frobisher, a woman who had dealt with so much in her life, educating hundreds of children, surviving a war and the loss of her husband and then supporting her teenage daughter bring up an illegitimate child. Her response was never going to be a simple attempt to placate me, her life experiences had taught her so much more about what makes people tick to know such a throwaway remark would never work. And so it was, as I sat in my Gran's garden that day, I first heard the word that terrified me more than imaginary aliens or runaway trains.

Prison.

The word came out in the middle of a lengthy explanation, but I didn't absorb anything else. My mind clung onto that single word, replaying it back to me, the echo blocking out all the rest of Gran's words, which floated past me unheard. She must have told me then about the crime he had committed, the length of sentence, all the whys and wherefores, but my ears were closed to all of it.

My sole focus was the image I had in my mind of my happy, smiling dad, in a bare prison cell, his face pressed up again the bars.

5

I can't remember if I ran out of the house in my slippers or sandals. Regardless of my footwear slowing me down, I ran as fast as I could and didn't stop running until I reached Imogen's house.

Imogen and her brother, Clive, were playing tennis in their back garden. I'd been to their house often enough to know I was welcome. I'd never used the front door, instead I ran down the side path, pushed open the wrought-iron gate and virtually hurled myself into Imogen's arms.

'You have to help me,' I wailed. I pulled her to one side, ignoring her brother's sigh of irritation that their game had been interrupted.

'What's the matter? Has something happened?'

'It's my dad.' It was only as I said the words that I started to realise I hadn't really listened to what Gran had told me. I ploughed on regardless. 'I think he's in prison.'

My voice dropped to a whisper as I realised where I was and who might be listening. As a local magistrate, Mr Rutherford would be loath for Imogen to be friends with the daughter of a convict. If he heard the truth about my dad, I would be banned from their home forever.

Imogen led me away to the bottom end of the garden, beyond a row of sycamore trees. We sat on a bench that had been fashioned from an old tree trunk.

'What's your dad done? Why has he been sent to prison?'

I told her what little I knew, which was almost nothing.

'You know he always comes to visit around my birthday and you know this year he didn't visit at all.' There was no need for me to remind her of those months when I plagued her with my fears of car crashes and aliens.

'He came last month though. You said he was going to Greece.'

Confronted with Imogen's doubts I started to feel less sure. But after a moment's hesitation, I ploughed on.

'I'm going to find him, Gen.'

'How?'

An image of the Brooke Bond tin floated into my mind. The 'rainy day' was here, even though the sun was shining. As I sat beside my friend, I formulated a plan. I would creep back into the house, take the tin and its contents and use it to buy a train ticket to Brighton. Just once I'd heard Brighton mentioned in connection with Dad. It was after his last visit, when Mum and Gran were bemoaning his lack of commitment.

'He's got himself caught up with a crowd of layabouts, arty types, musicians and all sorts,' Mum had said. 'Brighton is full of them.'

'You're going to steal from your Mum?' Imogen's words made me refocus.

'It's not stealing. That money is there for emergencies. Well, this is an emergency.'

'How far do you think you'll get? Won't people wonder what you're doing on a train on your own?'

'I'll tell them I'm going to visit a relative, which will be the truth.'

Now I had a plan I didn't want to delay.

'I wish I could come with you, but Dad would kill me. I'd be grounded for weeks.'

I stood and faced my friend. 'I have to go now, Gen. Wish me luck.'

'Don't go, Libby. I have a bad feeling about this.'

I gave her a hug and ran off through the gate at the bottom of her garden, which led onto a bridleway and then onto the road.

Getting into my house and out again, with the Brooke Bond tin safe in my hands – all without being seen – was going to be a challenge. As it was a weekend there was no point in waiting for Mum to go to work. She rarely did a Saturday night shift, and even then Gran would always be around. But on this occasion the weather would be my ally. It was too hot for baking or household chores. Gran would be tending her garden and there was an outside chance she would have persuaded Mum to help her.

It was only an hour or so since I'd run out of the house, not enough time for either of them to be fretting too much about me. They probably guessed I'd gone to Imogen's and soon I would return, having calmed down.

There was a spot just to the right of our front path where I could see through to the back garden, while being hidden by a large hydrangea bush. I hovered there for a few moments and saw Gran pruning some roses, with Mum beside her holding out a trug to take the blooms that were almost finished flowering. I crept down the path, pushed open the front door, grabbed the Brooke Bond tin from the kitchen windowsill and ran out again, leaving the front door ajar so that the noise of closing it wouldn't alert anyone.

However, I hadn't reckoned on the noise from the tin. The coins rattled around with each step I took. Emptying the tin and putting the coins in my pockets, would be just as noisy. Instead, I took my handkerchief from my skirt pocket and stuffed it into the tin, pressing it down hard so that the coins were protected from moving.

The bus driver cast me a strange look when I opened the tin and counted out the bus fare. So, as soon as I arrived at the railway station I found a quiet bench and emptied the tin onto my lap. I was tempted to offer the change to the man behind the counter at the railway buffet, in return for notes, but decided against it. Instead, I picked out the sixpences and shillings and shoved all the copper back into the tin, securing it once more with my handkerchief.

Having bought the train ticket and waited a half hour for the train, I had time to plan my next move. When I arrived in Brighton I would ask around for the prison address and hopefully another bus ride would take me right to the door.

Once I was on the train, I stared out of the window and conjured up an image of Dad's face. His smile would be guaranteed once he saw me. It would be worth all the telling off and harsh words I'd get from Mum and Gran once I was back home. I knew I would have to go home sometime, but at least I would have seen Dad and maybe I could persuade them to let me visit him in prison once a month, even once a week, until the end of his sentence.

These thoughts kept me occupied for the hour-long journey and helped me ignore the occasional glances I got from other passengers who seemed intrigued by the idea of a young girl sitting on her own in a railway carriage, clinging tightly to a Brooke Bond tin.

Arriving in Brighton, I took my time leaving the train, letting everyone else off first. In truth, now I was here, I felt daunted by the task ahead. I walked slowly towards the ticket barrier, not noticing that the two uniformed men standing beside the railway officials were not railway staff, but policemen. As I stepped forward and handed my ticket over, one of the policemen put his hand on my shoulder.

'Elizabeth Frobisher?'

I shrugged his hand away. 'No one calls me Elizabeth, I'm Libby.'

The uniformed presence didn't faze me, in fact, I saw it as an opportunity. 'I hope you can help me, officer. I need to find the prison. My dad is being kept there and it's very important I visit.'

Both policemen seemed to find my announcement amusing. Then the tallest of the two stopped chuckling and rearranged his face to take on a frown of disapproval.

'Your mother is very worried about you. We need to get you home.'

'I can't go home until I've seen my dad.' I pulled away from the officer, but he put his hand out and pulled me back.

'We don't know anything about your father, Miss, but we do know you've caused quite a panic.'

They marched me off to a waiting police car and I sat in silence for much of the drive home.

There was just one question I asked, for which I already knew the answer.

'How did you know where to find me? It was Imogen, wasn't it?'

'Your friend did the right thing. She was worried about you. She told her father and Mr Rutherford rang us. A lass like you, disappearing like that, well it gave your friends and family quite a fright.'

I reflected on his words. With hindsight, I could see that I had done to Mum and Gran what Dad had done to me.

6

And so, on that blisteringly hot Saturday, halfway through my tenth year, I learned some truths about my dad.

Gran made herself scarce, leaving Mum to tell me the story.

We sat together at the kitchen table, with the back door and the window wide open to encourage a through draught. Mum started at the point that for her was the beginning, before she met Adam, but not before she had experienced heartache.

'You remember I told you I'd volunteered during the war? I was only a few years older than you are now. I used to visit the hospital, sit at the bedside of wounded soldiers and help them write letters to their loved ones.'

'Because they couldn't write?' I asked, trying to get to grips with events that meant little to me.

'Because they couldn't see. Some of them had lost their sight altogether, for others it was temporary. They were the lucky ones. Anyway, there was this one lad, John, and well, I supposed I developed a bit of a crush on him. He was older than me, but he used to make me laugh and when he was discharged from hospital, we stayed friends.'

'Friends?' I knew enough to appreciate there were all sorts of friendships. Maybe this John was really my father and not Adam. I was leaping ahead, jumping to ridiculous conclusions.

'Just friends,' she said, the beginning of a smile creeping across her face. 'Then John re-joined his battalion and was posted back to the front. He promised to write.'

'And did he?'

The smile faded from her face, replaced with something much sadder.

'Not long after he returned to France he was killed. I didn't get to hear about it for ages. As far as the army and his family were concerned, I was just an acquaintance. A few months passed with no letters, so I visited his mum and she told me.'

Her shoulders sagged and I wondered how the story would go from here. So far she hadn't even mentioned Dad and, as sad as it was that John had died, I didn't know anything about him. I couldn't feel sorry about someone I'd never met. I wriggled on the chair, hoping she would sense my impatience.

'I vowed to have nothing more to do with boys. I carried on volunteering at the hospital, but made sure I only helped the older soldiers. It got me into trouble with the Ward Sister a few times, but there were plenty of other volunteers who were more than happy to swap with me. They snapped up the chance to sit beside the bed of the young soldiers and airmen.

'Then one day, I went to the bedside of an airman whose plane had been shot down, just as he was returning to base. His face had been badly burned, his hands too. He was dictating a letter to me, when Adam arrived. It turned out that Adam was his son.'

'And you fell in love, just like that?'

I wanted to believe in a fairy tale ending, even though I already knew there wasn't one.

'I didn't speak to Adam the first time I saw him. He arrived and I left. Then a few days later your gran had a telegram to say that your granddad had been killed.'

I looked down at Mum's hands, which were clasped tightly together. I was beginning to wish she hadn't started the story, as it seemed to have nothing but sadness about it. I'd had visions of my parents being young, carefree and yet it seemed the beginning of their relationship was overshadowed by brutal heartache.

'I went to the hospital that day, but I didn't go inside,' she continued. 'I sat on one of the benches in the hospital grounds. It was springtime, but not quite warm enough to be without a jacket. When Adam saw me shivering he sat beside me and put his arm round me and then I started to cry and couldn't stop. I cried for John and for my dad and for all the poor people in the hospital who had had their lives altered forever by the blessed war.'

'And then you fell in love?'

It must have been something about the persistent simplicity of my questions that made her smile.

'No, darling, we never fell in love. Not really. But Adam was able to make the sun shine, even when the clouds threatened to overshadow everything.'

'With his smile?'

'Yes, with his smile. He refused to talk about anything sad or negative. He made me believe that life could be good, that it would be good again, despite all that had happened.'

'Didn't you want to get married?'

All the time Mum had been speaking the kitchen tap had been dripping, providing a repetitive soundtrack to her story, like that of a ticking clock. She stood and moved over to the sink, attempting to tighten the tap closed.

'New washer, I'm thinking.' She was almost speaking to herself, as though she had forgotten I was there. 'Adam isn't the marrying kind,' she said, as if she was repeating a statement that had been told to her.

Perhaps that's what Dad had given as his excuse. But hearing her say it made me angry. *What is the marrying kind, anyway? Can someone just choose a life of irresponsibility, even when the result is that someone else has to take up all the slack?*

'And now he's in prison and I'm pleased, because he's let you down, he's let us down, so he deserves it,' I said, with emphasis.

I had transferred my allegiance, just like that. Since the age of three, when Adam was first introduced to me, I had idolised him. I'd forgiven him all his absences and blamed my mum for everything I considered wrong with my life. But now I understood a different truth, one where my dad had taken advantage of my mum at a time when she was grieving and vulnerable. Then, once he'd had his way with her, he'd left her high and dry. With Gran's help Mum had made a good life for me and in return I'd been sullen and ungrateful.

I moved towards Mum, who was still at the kitchen sink, but with her back to me. I wrapped my arms around her waist.

'I'm so sorry, Mum.' The words weren't enough to undo my inconsiderate behaviour, but I hoped she appreciated that they represented a turning point.

She swivelled round to face me, putting her hands on my shoulders. 'Oh, Libby, you don't have to apologise, none of this is your fault. And, darling, you've somehow got the wrong end of the stick. Your dad isn't in prison.'

7

I was ten years old, going on fifteen. I thought I knew everything, when of course, I knew very little and understood even less.

When Mum took me by the hand and led me out into the back garden, I asked no questions. Instead, I replayed the thoughts I'd had over the previous few hours. I felt as though I'd been on a roundabout that had been spinning too fast, with possibilities coming into view and then vanishing again.

As we approached, Gran was kneeling on the ground beside one of the vegetable beds. She appeared to be picking insects from a crop of broad beans.

'Are you all sorted now?' Gran said, continuing to concentrate on her task.

'We are far from sorted,' Mum said. 'It seems that Libby has misunderstood what you tried to tell her about Adam and prison.'

Gran took her gardening gloves off and eased herself up to standing.

'It's best I leave you with your Gran and this time, Libby, don't interrupt, don't fly off the handle, just listen.' Mum emphasised the final word, squeezed my hand and then returned to the kitchen.

'Come on, let's take a walk,' Gran said. 'We need to find some shade.'

I followed her down the side path, onto the road that led to a nearby playground. There were several children using the swings and roundabout, watched over by a couple of women sitting on the only available bench.

Gran nodded towards the far side of the play area where a narrow track led up into a small clump of beech trees.

She sat and leaned up against the trunk of one of them. I knelt beside her and started picking at the grass and clover around me.

Since we'd left home Gran hadn't spoken a word. I guessed she was working out what to tell me, as well as how to phrase it, given that her first attempt at an explanation had gone so awry.

'Your father is not a bad man,' she said, a note of caution in her voice. 'But he's easily led.'

She paused and for a moment I wondered if that was it, the sum total of her analysis of my dad. I took a breath, about to rise to his defence, when she put a hand up to stop me.

'Remember, Libby, no interruptions.'

I covered my mouth with one hand, making the point that I was heeding her instruction.

'After your granddad died, well, your mum took it very hard. She loved her father very much and for a while she went a bit wild.'

I couldn't imagine Mum being 'wild' and my questioning expression probably indicated as much.

'Well, that's when she got together with Adam and pretty soon after that she discovered she was expecting you. At first she didn't want to tell Adam. She was angry with him, but in truth I believe she was more angry with herself for letting it happen.'

She glanced sideways at me as though checking I was still listening. Seeing that I was riveted to the spot, she continued.

'I persuaded her to tell him. He came to the house and I left them to talk together in the sitting room. I hovered in the kitchen and am not ashamed to say I listened in. As soon as your Mum explained how she was in the family way, it all went quiet. I'd met Adam a few times and I always thought him to be a nice lad, but a bit of a dreamer. I anticipated he would struggle with the news, but couldn't be sure how he would deal with it. After a while I heard him shout out, I'm going to be a dad, I can't believe it. There was real joy in his voice, but your mum was crying as she told him and it was as though he was oblivious to all the implications. She started to spell it out to him, explaining that it would be impossible, they weren't married, they had nowhere to live and little or no money. He went quiet then and a few moments later he came through to the kitchen. He told me he was sorry for all the trouble he'd caused, but that he would make everything right.'

'Were you angry with him?'

'Darling, I know all about the temptations young men and women face. I was young myself once, remember?'

I realised what Gran was referring to and it made me blush. What little I knew about how a baby was made I had read in a book at the library. I couldn't imagine Mum and Adam having sex, it was such an intimate act and yet she could hardly bear to be in the same room as him now. None of it made any sense.

'Adam wanted to provide for your mum, which meant he needed money. He was seventeen, the same age as your mum, with no trade to speak of and no immediate opportunity to earn the money that would be needed. Unfortunately, at the time he was part of a group of lads who were always in trouble with the police. Libby, there's no easy way to say this, but Adam committed a crime.'

I realised I'd been holding my breath. As I took a gulp of air, it made me cough and Gran rubbed my back for a moment while I regained control enough to speak.

'And that's when he went to prison?'

She nodded. 'He helped some friends to rob a newsagent, he was the one who drove the car. Of course, they all got caught. It wasn't as though a lot of careful planning went into it. They broke into the shop on a Friday night and most of the takings had been banked that day anyway. There was little or nothing left in the till. But the shopkeeper and his wife lived above the shop, and the poor man came down when he heard noises. One of Adam's friends hit out at the man and that's why the sentence was more harsh than it might have been.'

'Is that why I didn't get to meet Dad until I was three?'

The shafts of light that shone down through the branches of the tree were making patterns on the ground. I trailed my finger across them, remembering that first meeting with Adam and how it must have been for him. I wondered whether Mum had visited him while he was in prison. Maybe she wrote to him, perhaps he had a photo of me that he pinned up on the wall of his cell.

'Your mum told Adam that she would never let him be fully involved in your life. He could visit, but nothing more than that. She didn't trust him, you see.'

'But he just wanted to help. To get some money so we could have been a real family. What's so wrong with that?' I stood and turned away from Gran so she couldn't see the tears that were starting to fall. 'Isn't everyone allowed to make one mistake?' I bent forward, focused on the ground, so that my words came out as little more than a whisper.

'If he'd taken a different path, got himself a steady job, perhaps it would have been different,' Gran said. 'But ever since he's been out of prison he's just drifted. I don't think he'll ever be ready to settle.'

'What's so good about being "settled" anyway? It's just boring. Doing the same thing every day, never having any adventures. At least Dad has adventures.'

These revelations about Dad meant a shift in all the co-ordinates that had framed my life until that point. I thought I understood what it meant for something to be right or wrong, good or bad. Instead, I was discovering there were a whole host of other levels in-between. I felt as if I was standing on a patch of sinking sand, trying to grab hold of something strong and reliable and realising there was nothing or no one within reach.

<h1 style="text-align:center">8</h1>

Nearly six months passed before I saw Dad again. The half-term holidays, Shrove Tuesday and my birthday, all coincided again that year and Mum promised me pancakes for breakfast. Since the lengthy discussions that had taken place that summer, I almost hoped Dad wouldn't turn up. When I thought about him I felt so conflicted. It was as though I was sitting on the fulcrum of a see-saw, my allegiances constantly tipping from one side to the other. My dad had made mistakes, but so had my mum. Blame could be meted out in equal measure. Some days I was angry with him, ready to hurl accusations at him about his treatment of Mum and of me. Other days it was Mum I was mad at, for holding on to regret and resentment for so long. I wanted someone to blame, only then could I resolve my confused emotions.

On the day of my birthday I woke early, listening to Mum moving around downstairs. I pictured the three presents that I knew were waiting for me. Imogen had given me a gift, beautifully wrapped in crimson paper, tied with a matching ribbon. I'd been trying to guess its contents, weighing it in my hand and shaking it to see if it rattled. I'd convinced myself it might be a paperweight because it was so heavy, but I couldn't imagine why she would buy such a thing. A paperweight was the kind of gift she might choose for her dad, but seemed an odd choice for her eleven-year-old friend.

Beside Imogen's present was something large and squashy from Gran (my guess was a hand-knitted jumper) and from Mum a shape that could only be a book. The Lord of the Rings had been published just the year before and I had spoken about nothing else. Gran told me to be sensible and wait for it to reach the library's shelves, but I still held out hope that Mum had bought me a copy. When I think about it now, I am embarrassed at just how naïve I was. She could no more afford a hardback copy of such a tome than she could afford to treat herself to a new coat and it would be the latter she needed, far more than I needed yet another fantastic tale to feed my imagination.

I padded down to the kitchen, my slippers trodden down at the back because I could never be bothered to put my whole foot inside. Mum was already back from work and was starting to make the pancake batter, beating the eggs in such a way that suggested her night shift had been difficult. She had her back to me as I came into the kitchen. I stood and watched her, willing her to turn around. My insides were bubbling with anticipation. I wanted everything to be exciting, but as I looked around the kitchen the bubbles within me lost their fizz. Although I couldn't see Mum's expression, I could tell her mood from the slump in her shoulders.

It was as Mum moved towards the larder to get the flour that the back door flung open and in walked my dad. He was burnished bronze from the Aegean sun, the guitar that was slung over his shoulder suggesting that he'd been learning more about music than fishing. I ran towards him and threw my arms around his waist, all angry thoughts washed away as I breathed in his smell. It was a mix of cigarette smoke and sweat and yet there was a sweetness about it. Gran smelled of lavender, Mum of hospital antiseptic, but Dad's smell was unique. After all, he was the only man I'd ever got close enough to notice their smell. Mr Rutherford and the male teachers at school certainly didn't count.

There was a mumbled Hello from Mum, who barely turned to look at him, but any intended snub washed over him as he released me from our hug, standing back to look at me.

'You're at least an inch taller. Any more growing and you'll have caught me up,' he said, that smile making all his words sound lively and full of humour.

'We're having pancakes,' I said, pointing to the bowl that Mum was still holding.

'Of course you are. Enough for me, do you reckon?' He pulled a chair out from the table and sat, his long legs stretching out in front of him. I stood beside him and plucked at one of the guitar strings.

'Will you teach me to play?'

The scene unfolding in our kitchen that morning was a continuation of years of unspoken resentment. Mum's opinion of Adam was evident and had barely changed in eleven years.

The last time I saw my dad I had watched him walk up the path, away from me and towards a different life. I couldn't decide whether he was lucky or selfish. I'd had two postcards from him, which Mum would have ripped up and put in the bin if I hadn't got to the postman first. I'd pinned the cards on my bedroom wall, beside my posters of Elvis and James Dean. I'd lie on my bed and imagine Dad splashing about in the azure sea, or rowing out in a little boat to catch fish that he would cook over an open fire on the white sandy beach.

'What was it like? Did you learn to fish like you said you would?' I wanted to be transported out of the kitchen in Tidehaven and onto a Greek island.

'It's the most beautiful place I've ever seen, crystal blue seas, sand so hot that some days you can barely walk on it. And plenty of cheap food and free love.'

I blushed and moved away from him. It was as if he was taunting Mum. It wasn't fair; she didn't deserve that.

'And now my Primrose is eleven years old, almost a young lady,' he said, ignoring my disapproving expression.

'How about those pancakes then? Are they ready yet?' Gran said, walking into the kitchen and giving a cursory nod to Dad. She stood beside Mum who still had her back towards us.

We hadn't seen Dad for over a year and yet it was as though he had just returned from a trip to the local shops. They showed no interest in what he had been doing, where he had been, or why he had chosen to return.

'Libby, get the lemons from the fridge, will you?' Mum moved over to the cooker and turned on the gas. Dad and I watched as the butter sizzled in the frying pan, the smell of it smoky and rich. Gran set the table with four places, and then sat opposite Dad, her expression blank. She started to hum a tune I didn't recognise, but Dad clearly did as he picked up the guitar and started strumming an accompaniment. If someone had walked into the kitchen at that moment they might have thought we were a relaxed, happy family, sharing a breakfast routine that was as familiar to us as breathing. Instead there was a tension in the atmosphere that hung over each of us.

Mum poured the first batch of batter into the frying pan and jiggled it around until it covered the whole base of the pan. She left it for a few minutes until it was set, then just as she went to flip the pancake over with a spatula, Dad jumped up and grabbed the pan from her.

'Hang on,' he said, 'aren't you going to toss it in the air?'

Mum pushed him away, he grabbed the pan and she grabbed it back. Then I ducked as Mum hurled the pan and its contents across the kitchen. The pan landed on the floor with a resonant crack; the pancake splattered beside it.

We were all shocked into silence for a few moments. Gran was the first to speak.

'That wasn't your brightest moment,' she said, bending down to scoop the pieces of pancake back into the pan.

'Missed your target completely, I'd say,' Dad said, half a smile on his face.

'You think you can waltz into our lives, then waltz out again, with no thought as to how it affects Libby. I'm sick of it, sick of you.' Mum's voice was low and controlled, as though it was the only part of her she could control.

'I thought you were angry about the pancakes.' Dad's voice was as calm as ever.

'Audrey,' Gran said, putting her hand gently onto Mum's shoulder. 'You sit and I'll sort out the breakfast.'

Birthday or no birthday, it looked as though we wouldn't be having pancakes that day.

Mum pulled one of the chairs away from the table and sat on the very edge of it. She was still wearing her nurse's uniform, but had an overall over the top of it. Everything about her was sensible, her flat lace-up shoes, her hair pulled back into a tight ponytail. By contrast, everything about Dad was casual, his white tee-shirt, blue jeans and scruffy black jacket, his hair tousled as though he hadn't long woken up.

'I want you to go now,' Mum told him.

'No,' I said, with more confidence than I felt. 'It's my birthday and I want Dad here. And I want you two to be nice to each other. You must have liked each other once. Otherwise I wouldn't be here.'

I paused, hoping my words weren't going to make the situation worse. When no one spoke, I continued.

'Can't you just be friends, for my sake?'

All three adults looked at me. Then Dad spoke.

'How about I come back tonight for tea? See if we can't salvage something out of the day. For Libby's sake.'

'You like to think all you do, all you've ever done, is for Libby's sake.' Mum almost spat the words out and I felt as though my name was being tossed around, used as an excuse for blame and counter blame.

Dad picked up the guitar and ruffled my hair with his hand. 'I'll come back later, Primrose. Maybe I'll even play you a tune on this.' He strummed a few notes on his guitar, then turned and left, as suddenly as he'd arrived.

I retreated to my bedroom, a lead weight in my stomach replacing the fizzing bubbles that I had started the day with. I could hear the low murmur of conversation between Mum and Gran, but I wasn't interested in what they had to say. My birthday was spoiled. It would be a day I remembered for all the wrong reasons.

I stayed up in my bedroom for most of the day, Mum came up several times, trying to entice me to at least open my presents. I wrote out a sign and taped it to my bedroom door.

You have ruined my life.

It was an overstatement, of course, but at that moment it was how I felt.

Later that afternoon I wandered downstairs. Gran had gone to the shops, perhaps taking time away from the tension and Mum was sitting in the front room, her eyes closed. She had changed into a crimson frock that I had never seen before. Her hair was different too, falling loose around her face, softening everything about her. I sat beside her and waited for her to open her eyes.

'Hello,' she said and with that simple greeting it was as if all that had gone before was forgotten.

It was evening by the time Dad returned. He wandered into the kitchen, clutching his guitar, as though the morning's events had never happened. I saw his gaze go momentarily to the kitchen counter, where my three presents remained unwrapped.

Gran had taken the bus to Tamarisk Bay to visit a friend. Mum was sitting at the kitchen table, her sewing basket opened and several pairs of my socks awaiting darning. She had taken a rare night off from the hospital. Perhaps she had planned it so because of my birthday, nevertheless I was pleased she was there to see that Dad had kept his promise to return.

When he walked into the kitchen she kept her head down, her eyes focused on the strand of wool she was attempting to thread through the needle. The morning's events had left me feeling so confused that even now, with Dad standing there in front of me, I couldn't shake off my discomfort.

'We've had our tea,' I said.

'But you've not opened your presents, Primrose. And here's another one for you.' He handed me a long, thin box. There was no wrapping, but that was usual for Dad's gifts. I looked at Mum, willing her to look up. I wanted her to see me open the present, to acknowledge that Dad cared about me enough to buy me something special; because I guessed it was special, even before I looked inside. I slid the cover off the box to reveal a recorder. Exciting possibilities opened up before me, I could have lessons at school, maybe even play in the end of term concert. I would be a musician.

'How about it, then? You on the recorder, me on the guitar, we could form our own band,' Dad said, his smile back in place.

'I love it,' I said, throwing my arms around his waist. 'Thank you so much. It's the best present.'

I took the recorder out of its velvet-lined box and put it to my lips. The first sound to come out of it sounded more like the blast on a ship's horn, rather than anything resembling music.

'Look, Mum. What do you think? Isn't it great?' I thrust the recorder at her, forcing her to look at it.

She put her sewing down and took the recorder from me.

'Blow gently into it, Libby, like this,' she said. She started to play a tune, which within seconds I recognised.

'It's happy birthday, you're playing happy birthday.' I wanted to dance around the kitchen table. Dad began to clap along to the music, laughing, and looking at Mum with such tenderness that I thought for a moment it would all be alright, that everything was possible.

Then she stopped playing and put the recorder back into its box.

'I learned to play at school, when I was about your age,' she said. 'But I never had my own recorder, you're a lucky girl, Libby.'

She gave a polite nod to Dad and then, 'Will you stay for a cup of tea?'

The three of us sat around the kitchen table, while Dad described his trip to the Greek island of Hydra. He told us about the people he met, explaining how they were living in a kind of commune.

'There were artists, poets, musicians, everyone just hanging out.'

There were pauses in his story and I guessed what Mum would be thinking. She had no time to 'hang out'. Her night shifts at the hospital left her too tired to enjoy her days off, and though she was still only twenty-eight years old, she looked middle-aged.

As Dad spoke, I drifted off into thoughts of Dad and me spending evenings together, just 'hanging out'. Maybe he could earn money as a musician and Mum wouldn't have to work as much. Maybe he'd move in with us and we could be like a real family.

'Why did you come back?' Mum's question broke into my thoughts, turning the warmth of possibilities into the cold reality of the here and now.

Dad picked up his guitar and started strumming.

'You're going back, aren't you?' she said.

'You could come with me, you and Primrose. You'd love it there, I know you would.' He spoke as though it was all possible. We could stuff some clothes into a rucksack and set off together on an adventure. He had travelled down by bus, the fare just a few pounds and life on the island was so cheap that he earned all he needed by working evenings in a bar.

I was ready to run upstairs and grab a few things and leave at that moment. I wanted to make Mum agree, even though I knew she wouldn't.

She didn't reply. We would never go to live on Hydra. Dad would never come to live with us.

That evening was the first of several visits Dad made to us over the next few months. During those treasured moments we spent together, he taught me three chords on the guitar, and congratulated me when I played my first tune on the recorder. But then, before the end of the summer of my eleventh year, he was off again, travelling on the '*Magic Bus*', returning to Hydra to live among people who thought as he did, folk who believed a simple life was a happy life.

9

There are at least two ways of making pancakes. You can use a spatula and turn your perfectly formed pancake over, in a controlled and safe way, or you can toss it high in the air, without fear. If you are lucky you will catch it, but sometimes you might just hold the pan a little too far to the left or the right, and your pancake does not end up as perfect as you hoped.

Who would have thought the simple action of making pancakes could teach us something about life? I can see now that there are people who are happy to throw caution high into the air, leaving it to random chance as to whether events land well or badly, and others who cling to the safety of that spatula.

I am twenty now and I've spent hours, weeks, months and years trying to understand people. I've learned there are many different ways to live and labels, such as 'good', 'bad', 'right', or 'wrong', have no value when it comes to describing the choices people make.

I can see now that for much of my childhood Mum chose the safe route through her life, using the spatula of work and responsibility to control the outcome. Perhaps from the day she was told her father had died she was full of fear, clutching first to Adam in her desire to be safe, and then to the routine that became our life together.

By contrast, Dad saw no obstacles. Whatever way the events in his life landed suited him just fine.

Of course, I appreciate nothing is that simple. It was only because Mum took on the responsibility of caring for me that Dad was free to live the life he chose.

I don't blame either of them, not anymore.

Dad is still in Hydra, nearly ten years on. There's an open invitation for me to visit. He writes often, mostly poems that could just as easily be lyrics for the songs I imagine him singing, strumming his guitar, while he sits on a Greek beach and studies the sunset. One day I might surprise him and turn up there and let him see his Primrose, all grown up.

Mum still works at the hospital, but mostly day shifts now, having been promoted to Ward Sister. We moved out to our own little house in Tamarisk Bay, where we listen to records most evenings, dancing around the kitchen to *Gerry and the Pacemakers* and the *Dave Clark Five*. We spend our days off seeking out bargains in the local boutiques and the funniest compliment we got the other day was when some chap thought we were sisters. It's not just the clothes that Mum wears, or the way she styles her hair, it's more than that. The frown lines have faded, replaced with tiny creases around the edges of her mouth from the smiles that come much more frequently.

Imogen visited the other day. She sat on my bed while she painted my nails the most delicate shade of pink.

'I was thinking about that time when you ran off,' she said, the bottle of nail varnish balanced on her lap, looking slightly precarious.

'Yeah, well, I've done some pretty stupid things in my time, but I was only ten years old, remember.'

'I kind of envied you.'

'There was nothing about my life to envy, you had a proper family, a beautiful house, even a tennis court.'

'Yeah, but it was all normal. Whereas you…'.

'Weird, is that what you're saying?' I went to pull my hand away from her, forgetting that she was still only midway through the manicure.

'Different. That's what I envied.'

'And you bought me that,' I pointed to the paperweight that was sat in the centre of my dressing table. 'I never understood what made you think I'd want a paperweight, until I realised it was really a globe.'

She let my hand drop and moved over to the dressing table, picking up the paperweight and running her fingers across the glass.

'I love how the whole world is etched out, as though you could just step from one country to another in a moment.'

'Maybe that's what we'll do one day, together.'

'What, walk around the world?' She did a twirl, holding the paperweight up above her head.

'Don't you dare drop it,' I said, momentarily flashing back to the moment in the kitchen all those years earlier, when Mum had thrown the frying pan across the kitchen, the pancake landing on the floor.

She put the globe down and moved across to my bookshelves.

'And your Mum bought you this that same year, didn't she?' She pulled out my treasured copy of *The Lord of the Rings*, flicking through it before handing it to me.

I opened the front cover and read aloud the words that Mum had written.

'All the adventures are out there just waiting for you to find them.'

'Do you think your Mum wishes she'd had more adventures?'

My reply was to shrug and look down at my part-painted nails.

'All I know is that everything is so much more complicated than I thought it was when I was ten years old,' I said, smiling.

'And more fun?' she said, taking my hand and slowly painting the remaining fingernails, while I hummed the only tune I'd mastered on my recorder, which now lay in my bedside drawer, beside my diary from 1951 and the faded photo of my dad.

MORE SUSSEX CRIME

The *Sussex Crime* stories are centered around the fictional seaside town of Tamarisk Bay. To date there are three novels in the series, which are set in the late 1960s, with young librarian and amateur sleuth, Janie Juke solving crimes and mysteries.

This is the third novella in the *Sussex Crime* series, where we meet some of the same folk who appear in the novels, but many years earlier.

The first novella is entitled, *Divided we Fall*, set during the Second World War. We learn about the exploits of Janie Juke's father, Philip, who is just a boy when the story unfolds.

In the second novella, *More than Ashes*, we meet schoolteacher Phyllis Frobisher, and her daughter Audrey. In the novels we meet Phyllis again. She is a great support to Janie Juke, and Audrey's daughter, Libby is an investigative journalist with a taste for adventure, who enjoys racing around Tamarisk Bay with her friend, Janie Juke, looking for clues and helping to solve mysteries.

And in this third novella, *Waiting for Sunshine,* we meet Phyllis, Audrey and Libby Frobisher once more. This time it is Libby's story we hear, long before she matures into the young woman we meet in the novels.

If you would like to read more about this whole cast of characters, then look out for the full-length novels in the series:

BOOK 1: **THE TAPESTRY BAG**
BOOK 2: **LOST PROPERTY**
BOOK 3: **THE INVISIBLE CASE**

All three novels are available as a trilogy here:
THE SUSSEX CRIME MYSTERIES: A Janie Juke trilogy

And if you would like to read more from Isabella Muir then take a look at this standalone novel:
THE FORGOTTEN CHILDREN - a mother's story about the search for her child

And these short story anthologies:
TWELVE AT CHRISTMAS - an anthology of twelve Christmas-themed short stories
IVORY VELLUM - an anthology of short stories

If you enjoyed this book, then you can help other readers to discover it too, by leaving a review on any of the online book review websites.

Thank you

PRAISE FOR THE SUSSEX CRIME SERIES

'This was a great find. A librarian turns to sleuthing in 1960s England. Janie Juke, an Agatha Christie enthusiast, is a very likeable protagonist. A real page turner. I've already bought the next book in the series… hoping there will be many more to come.'

'I got straight into the story … I really like the way the author depicted the 60s …I felt as if I was there!'

'Intriguing detective story with lovely period setting and interesting characters. I'm looking forward to seeing what Janie Juke solves next.'

'Loved every page and didn't want to put it down. Can't wait until the next one in the series.'

'Thoroughly enjoyable book. Kept me interested till the end. Looking forward to the next one.'

'The glimpses into WW2 are particularly good. Solid writing, great story, and Janie as a character is growing on me. I hope there are more in the series.'

ABOUT THE AUTHOR

Isabella rediscovered her love of writing fiction during two happy years working on and completing her MA in Professional Writing.

The setting for the *Sussex Crime* mystery series is based on the area where Isabella was born and lived most of her life. When she thinks of Tamarisk Bay she pictures her birthplace in St Leonards-on-Sea, East Sussex and its surroundings.

Aside from her love of words, Isabella has a love of all things caravan-like. She has enjoyed several years travelling in the UK and abroad. Now, Isabella and her husband run a small campsite in West Sussex.

You can discover more about Isabella's books and characters on her website, or download a free novella when you sign up for Isabella Muir's newsletter and you can follow Isabella on Twitter: **@SussexMysteries**